P9-CCB-085

Farmer Mack Measures His Pig

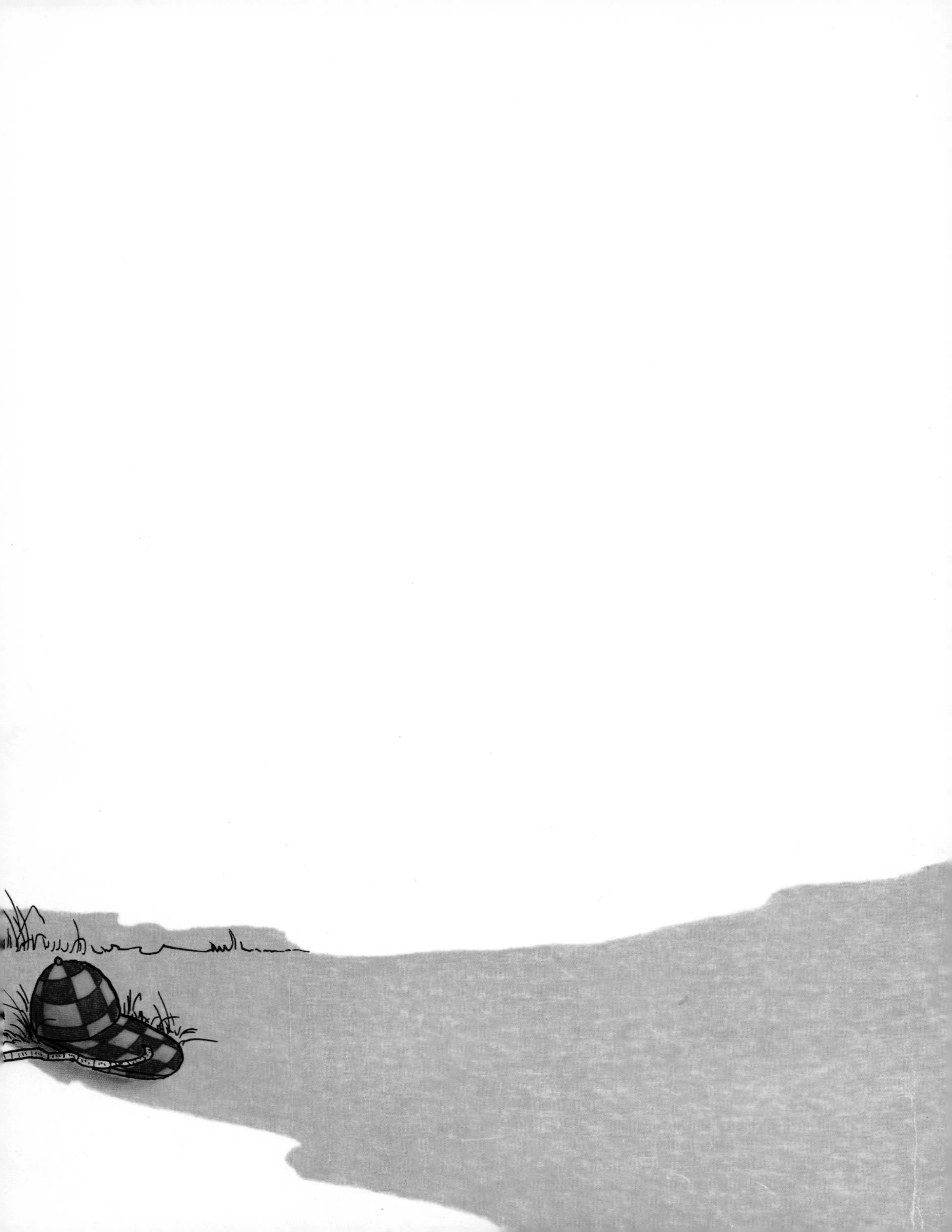

FARMER MACK MEASURES HIS PIG

by Tony Johnston · illustrated by Megan Lloyd

Harper & Row, Publishers
New York

For Ant Helen and Uncle Bob
with the caution:
Never enter a pig-calling contest
with an operatic soprano!
—T.J.

For Tom and his little pig, Squeak
—M.L.

Farmer Mack Measures His Pig

Printed in the United States of America. For information address Harper & Row Junior Books, 10 East 53rd Street, New York, N.Y. 10022. Published simultaneously in Canada by Fitzhenry & Whiteside Limited, Toronto.

Library of Congress Cataloging-in-Publication Data
Johnston, Tony.
Farmer Mack measures his pig.

Summary: Farmer Mack's attempts to measure his wonderfully fat pig create chaos on his farm.
[1. Pigs—Fiction. 2. Farms—Fiction]
I. Lloyd, Megan, ill. II. Title.
PZ7.J6478Far 1986 [E] 85-45253
ISBN 0-06-023017-7
ISBN 0-06-023018-5 (lib. bdg.)

1 2 3 4 5 6 7 8 9 10
First Edition

Farmer Mack was proud of his big pig, Goldie.
"I bet she's the roundest pig around," he thought.

One day Farmer Tubb came by with his enormous spotted pig, Hugh.

"Guess what," he said to Farmer Mack. He was itching to tell his news.

"Can't," replied Farmer Mack.

"Well, I just measured Hugh, and he's one hundred inches around! He's the fattest pig alive."

Farmer Mack burst out with a loud "PSHAW!" By that he meant lots of things, like "Oh, beans" and "Fiddle-faddle" and "Who are you trying to kid?"

"Yes, sir," said Farmer Tubb proudly. "Your pig's a midget next to my Hugh."

"Pooh," said Farmer Mack, as he took out a tape measure and walked up to Goldie.

"Hold still, Goldie girl," Farmer Mack said, "and we'll show that runt who's fattest."

Goldie had another idea.

She let out a loud *oink* and ran for the trees.

"Look at her go," said Farmer Tubb. "She's ashamed to be so skinny."

"Oh, corn," replied Farmer Mack.

Farmer Mack strolled after Goldie. He did not want to scare her and thin her out with running.

He sneaked up on tiptoe.

Goldie did not like to be sneaked up on.

She dashed through the chicken yard and disappeared from sight.

"She can't stand the idea of being measured and losing," said Farmer Tubb.

"Horse whiskers," Farmer Mack muttered. "Where is that pesky porker?"

A pink snout poked out from behind the barn.

"After her!" Farmer Mack yelled, forgetting his plan about no running.

Goldie raced into the house. Farmer Mack was right behind her.

Farmer Mack was fit to be tied.
He looked behind a flower pot.
Not there.

He looked in his favorite chair.
Not there.

He looked under the bed.

There was Goldie, wedged in tight.
"Ha!" shouted Farmer Mack. "I'll measure you now, you pink devil. You're one hundred five inches around or my grandmother is a walrus!"

Goldie squealed, squirmed wildly, lifted the bed into the air, and bolted out from under it.

The bed collapsed on Farmer Mack.

By now Goldie was back outside, digging up the garden.
Farmer Mack got an idea. He called his neighbors together.

"Good friends," he said, "we'll have a pig-calling contest. Whoever gets Goldie close enough for me to measure wins a prize. Who's starting?"

Farmer Cooper was.
"Here, piggy, piggy, piggy," he called.
The piggy kept on digging.

Farmer Cobb was next.
"Pig-o! Pig-o! Pig-er-ooooooooo!" he roared.
The pigerooo stayed put.

Finally Farmer Twillie banged on a metal dish with a spoon and bellowed, "Cornflakes! Cornflakes!" over and over.

Goldie was hungry from so much digging. She ran for the cornflakes.

While Goldie was busy gobbling, Farmer Mack was busy trying to measure her.

But a large white butterfly spooked her, and Goldie was off in a pink blur.

"Drat that hulking ham!" shouted Farmer Mack.

Goldie ran this way and that.

Farmer Mack ran that way and this.

Goldie got so excited...

she jumped up on the picnic table!
The farmers came running to grab her.
They scrambled onto the table—all on the same end!

The table tilted. Goldie slid down like a rock and sped off again.

"I give up," said Farmer Mack in disgust. "I can't measure my pig."

"Too bad," said Farmer Tubb.

"Yep," agreed Farmer Mack. "We can never prove that Goldie is fatter than Hugh. But at least we know one thing for sure."

"What?" Farmer Tubb asked.

"My pig can jump higher than yours."

"Oh, beans," declared Farmer Tubb. "Mine never even tried."

"Well, now's his chance," said Farmer Mack.

Farmer Tubb lined Hugh up with the picnic table.

"Jump," he said.

Hugh didn't budge.

"Up, boy, up!" he coaxed.

Hugh didn't twitch.

"Poor Hugh's too nervous to jump," Farmer Tubb explained. "He needs a soothing song."

So Farmer Tubb got his banjo and began to sing.

"I love my pig better than my wife.
He's the darlin' of my life.
Snores all night like a buffa-lo!
Doodle-noodle-doodle-oh!

"My pig smells sweet as a rose in June.
Feed him donuts from a spoon.
Hair is blue and his eyes are toooooooooo!
Doodle-noodle-doodle-ooh!"

Suddenly, Farmer Mack noticed that Goldie had her eyes shut and was smiling like a baby in a cradle.

"Keep playing," he told Farmer Tubb.

So Farmer Tubb kept on plunking and jingling.

Farmer Mack walked over to Goldie, slipped the tape measure around her middle, and measured her then and there.

"ONE HUNDRED INCHES!" he hollered.

That holler was so loud, it scared Hugh right out of his skin and up onto the picnic table.

"Now *there's* a jumper," said Farmer Tubb proudly.

"Well, pluck my chickens! It's a tie!" announced Farmer Mack.

"That's a fact," said Farmer Tubb. "We sure have two fine pigs."

"The best," said Farmer Mack.

Then everyone strolled home singing. And Goldie and Hugh followed right behind.

"My pig's as big as a railroad train.
Counts to ten and down again.
Eats his meals in a tux-e-do!
Doodle-noodle-doodle-oh!"